Horrible Harry's in love?

We watched Song Lee lower her hand into the springwater. She put the toothpick with the piece of liver in front of the frog.

Zap! The frog gulped all the liver.

The toothpick was clean!

Harry looked at the frog and then at Song Lee. "I'm in love," he whispered.

"With a frog?" I replied.

"No! With her."

I looked at Miss Mackle. "The teacher?"

"Doug," Harry whispered. "I'm in love with Song Lee."

I gulped some air like that frog gulped the liver. "Really?"

OTHER PUFFIN BOOKS ABOUT ROOM 2B

HORRIBLE HARRY'S SECRET

BY SUZY KLINE
Pictures by Frank Remkiewicz

Puffin Books

PUFFIN BOOKS
Published by the Penguin Group
Penguin Putnam Inc., 375 Hudson Street, New York, New York 10014, U.S.A.
Penguin Books Ltd, 27 Wrights Lane, London W8 5TZ, England
Penguin Books Australia Ltd, Ringwood, Victoria, Australia
Penguin Books Canada Ltd, 10 Alcorn Avenue, Toronto, Ontario, Canada M4V 3B2
Penguin Books (N.Z.) Ltd, 182-190 Wairau Road, Auckland 10, New Zealand

Penguin Books Ltd, Registered Offices: Harmondsworth, Middlesex, England

First published in the United States of America by Viking Penguin,
a division of Penguin Books USA Inc., 1990
Published in Puffin Books, 1992
Reissued 1998

7 9 10 8

THE LIBRARY OF CONGRESS HAS CATALOGED THE PREVIOUS
PUFFIN BOOKS EDITION AS FOLLOWS:
Kline, Suzy.
Horrible Harry's secret / by Suzy Kline;
pictures by Frank Remkiewicz. p. cm.
Summary: Horrible Harry falls in love with Song Lee, and Harry's
best friend, Doug, can't stand all that mush.
ISBN 0-14-032915-3
[1. Friendship—Fiction. 2. Schools—Fiction.] I. Remkiewicz,
Frank, ill. II. Title.
[PZ7.K6797Hr 1992] [Fic]—dc20 92-20288

This edition ISBN 0-14-130093-0

Printed in the United States of America
Set in Century Schoolbook

RL: 2.1

Dedicated to my class who had a water frog,
drew portraits, made a blue winter mural, and
most of all wrote wonderful stories!

Dana Camire

Kyle Lovely

Craig Crowley

Kelli Anne McIntire

Amber Donaldson

Kristofer Manulla

Karin Dubreuil

Edmond Moore

Joseph Fasciano

Steven Moore

Jennifer Ford

Jennifer Patrizi

Elena Forzani

Amy Pozzo

Michael Hawley

Jamie Seamon

Michael Hickey

Karl Sieburg

Travis Issac

Sunny Sikhounmeuang

Miranda Languell

Elizabeth Talbot

Jessica Light

Contents

Horrible Harry's Secret

Horrible Harry's Secret

When Song Lee brought a water frog to Room 2B, Harry flashed a big smile. "Neat-o!" he said.

Harry loves slimy things, hairy things, and creepy things. Harry loves anything horrible. I know—I'm his best friend, Doug.

We watched the teacher help Song Lee set the tank on the science table.

"Does your frog have a name?" Miss Mackle asked.

"Bong," Song Lee said softly.

Sidney laid his ruler on his desk so that eight inches of it were sticking out. Then he hit the end of it. "Bong! Bong! Bong!"

Harry held up his fist. "Don't you make fun of a frog's name."

"I'm just making good music," Sidney replied, bonging his ruler some more.

"Well, stop it!" Harry demanded.

"Make me, Harry the canary!"

"You call me that one more time and I'll . . ."

"You'll what?"

Harry put his fist next to Sidney's nose. "I'll punch you in the schnozzola."

"SCHNOZZOLA!" Sidney cackled.

Song Lee looked over at the boys and frowned.

"Is Bong a Korean name?" the teacher asked.

Song Lee nodded. "Bong Lee was my grandfather. I name my frog after him."

Miss Mackle smiled as she tapped the tank. "Welcome to Room 2B, Bong. Have you fed him today?"

"I will feed Bong now."

When Song Lee brought out a small white carton, we gathered around the table.

"What do you feed your water frog?" Sidney asked.

Song Lee opened the lid and carefully put a little piece of food on a toothpick. "Liver," she said.

"*Eeyew!*" Sidney groaned. "Liver smells."

Harry took a deep whiff. "Mmmm, liver for the water frog. Awesome!"

We watched Song Lee lower her hand into the springwater. She put the toothpick with the piece of liver in front of the frog.

Zap! The frog gulped all the liver.

The toothpick was clean!

Sidney held his nose and went back to his seat.

Harry looked at the frog and then at Song Lee. "I'm in love," he whispered.

"With a frog?" I replied.

"No! With her."

I looked at Miss Mackle. "The teacher?"

"Doug," Harry whispered. "I'm in love with Song Lee."

I gulped some air like that frog gulped the liver. "Really?"

Harry nodded. Then he showed his two rows of perfect white teeth. It was the biggest smile I'd ever seen.

"Don't tell anyone," Harry added.

"Your secret is safe with me," I said.

As I went back to my seat, I thought about it. Harry did some horrible things in second grade but *this* was the most horriblest of all. I wouldn't *dare* say a word to anyone else.

Harry did himself.

It was during a math test when Miss Mackle explained how to fill in bubbles marked *a,b,c,* or *d*—None of the above.

That was when Harry got the idea to send the note. I looked at it quickly and then passed it on to Song Lee.

Dear Song Lee
    Do you Like me ?
    a.   a little
    b.   some
    c.   a Lot
    d.   None of the above
I like you.
    ♡ Harry

Five minutes later, the note came back. I couldn't look at it. All this love business was making me sick.

When I looked at Harry after he read it, I wondered if *he* was sick, too. His head was on his desk.

Then it came to me. Song Lee must have marked *d*—None of the Above. Poor Harry.

As we walked home from school, Harry didn't say anything. He acted like he was going to cry.

Suddenly, someone jumped from behind us. "BOO!" Sidney shouted.

Harry turned around.

"Hi, Harry the canary. . . . Tweet! Tweet!"

Uh-oh, I thought. Sidney's schnozzola was in trouble. I watched Harry roll up his sleeves.

When Song Lee, Mary, and Ida came walking down the street, Harry looked up.

"Yeah, El Tweeto? What are you planning to do about it?"

"Shake your hand," Harry replied. "I like birds. I think it's neat the way they get worms."

Sidney jerked his hand away. He wanted to see if there was a worm squished in it.

There wasn't.

Sidney was safe. He shook Harry's hand. Song Lee looked over and waved. Harry waved back.

That was when the note dropped out of Harry's jacket pocket. I looked down on the sidewalk and read it:

Dear Harry,
    I will like you if you don't fight with Sidney.
    It is bad to fight.
    I know because my Grandfather Bong die in Korean war.

 Song Lee

No wonder Harry looked sad walking home. He felt bad about Song Lee's grandfather.

But he sure didn't feel bad now. He

was smiling at Song Lee and still shaking Sidney's hand.

There was no doubt about it.

Harry was in love.

How horrible could things get?

The Deadly
Snowdown

The next morning we had our first snowfall of the school year! There were two inches of white fluffy stuff all over the ground, parked cars, rooftops, tree branches, and South School!

"Let's make snowballs," I said.

"Yeah!" Harry agreed.

We sank to our knees in a snowbank

near the school ramp and started making them.

"Pack them down good," Harry said.

We made a dozen snowballs in no time. Then we made a second pile. "TWO DOZEN!" I shouted. "So, who's our *first* victim?"

Just then a man was coming up the street in a winter hat. It was pulled low over his forehead. We could just see the guy's eyes and nose.

"Ready to fire?" Harry shouted.

I held my arm in the air. "Ready!"

Suddenly, we heard a familiar voice. "*Bravissimo!* Our first snow!" It was our principal!

"Good morning, boys," he called out.

"Good morning, Mr. Cardini!" we replied. We dropped our snowballs to the ground.

As he whistled by, we fell back in the

snow. "Phew! What a close call," I said.

When I heard another voice coming down the street, I sat up. "It's Sidney! Get ready to fire!" I called out.

Harry shook his head. "I'm not fighting with Sidney anymore, remember?"

Now Sidney couldn't be the victim.

"If we don't fire these snowballs pretty soon," I said, "they'll melt!"

"Shhhh!" Harry said. "Here comes some more voices. Be ready to attack."

Three girls in winter caps and scarves and mittens walked down the ramp.

"Ready to fire!" I called.

"Forget it, Doug," Harry grumbled. "It's Mary and Ida but Song Lee is with them. I don't want to attack her."

Of course he wouldn't. Harry was in *love* with Song Lee.

"You're no fun anymore," I said.

"Yeah? Well, why don't we fire snow-balls on each other."

"But we're friends," I said.

Harry grinned. "We could pretend we're enemies."

I grinned back. "PREPARE FOR WAR!"

Harry handed me two snowballs. He took two snowballs for himself. "Did you ever see a cowboy do a showdown?"

"Sure. Lots of times on TV. The good cowboy has a showdown with the bad cowboy."

"Well, we're going to do it just like they do, only we're calling it a snow-down."

"A snowdown?"

"You're the good cowboy, and I'm . . ." Harry growled, ". . . the *bad* cowboy. Stand back-to-back and take four paces.

After four paces, we turn and fire two shots!"

"Got it!"

As we stood back-to-back, I held one snowball in each hand. They were icy cold.

We started counting, "One. . . . Two. . . . Three. . . . FOUR!"

We turned around and aimed at each other.

SPLISH!
SPLAT!
WHISH!
WHOOSH!
Harry got me on the top of my head
and in the back. I nailed him in the
shoulder and stomach. We both fell

down laughing in the snow.

"You're dead!" I said.

"*You're* dead!" Harry said.

Suddenly, the school bell rang. We jumped to our feet. "We're BOTH dead!" I shouted. Quickly, we ran down the ramp like two downhill skiers.

The Red Foil Gift

As we raced across the playground, something fell out of Harry's pocket. It was a present wrapped in red foil paper and red ribbon.

"Who's that for?"

Harry flashed a big smile. "For Song Lee. But I have to find out if she really likes me first, before I give it to her."

Harry picked up the red gift and

we ran into the school building.

"Boys and girls," Miss Mackle said, as we rushed to our seats. "I thought we would celebrate our first big snowfall with an art workshop *all* morning."

Everyone clapped and cheered. Harry and I whistled. Our hands were frozen stiff.

"I mixed some blue paint, and cut a long strip of butcher paper. You can find a spot and start painting a wonderful winter mural that celebrates the Christmas and Hanukkah season!"

"Just one color of paint?" Mary complained.

"The blue color will give the mural a frosty look. You'll see, Mary."

Mary was still frowning. "Can we work with a friend?"

"If you like," the teacher replied.

Mary, Ida, and Song Lee huddled together.

"Okay," Miss Mackle said. "Everyone move their desks and chairs so you have lots of space to lie down and paint on the floor."

Harry pushed his desk over by the window and then he walked up to Sidney. "Do you want to do a snow picture together?"

Sidney took a step back. "Do you?"

"Sure, come on, Sid," Harry said, taking a carton of blue paint.

I was glad they didn't ask me to join them. Harry and Sidney working together? That was trouble.

Miss Mackle noticed right away. "I'm glad to see you boys bury the hatchet. It's time you got along!"

Harry and Sidney looked at each other. Then they giggled and started painting.

I didn't want any part of their plan. I stuck to my own. I made a picture of the snowdown Harry and I had before school. Song Lee and Ida and Mary were painting themselves in a big toboggan going down a hill.

I noticed Song Lee would stop and smile over at Harry and Sidney. Harry grinned back.

When Miss Mackle strolled by, she stopped by my work. "Hmmm. . . . Do I know those two boys throwing snowballs at each other?"

I laughed.

She did, too.

When she came to Harry and Sid-

ney's work, she stopped laughing. "What are you doing?"

Everyone gathered around to see what the boys had painted.

"A CEMETERY!" everyone shouted. "Look at the tombstones!"

Miss Mackle put her hands on her hips. "It is not Halloween, boys. We are supposed to be celebrating Christmas and Hanukkah, the season of peace and love."

Harry started to speak just as Mr. Cardini waltzed into the room. "A magnificent mural! Bravo!"

When he walked over and looked at the cemetery scene, he scratched his head. "Hmmmm, can you tell me about

your part of the mural, boys? Why did you paint a grave and *what* did you bury?"

"An axe!" Harry replied.

"An axe?"

"We buried the hatchet," Sidney grinned. "Harry and I are friends now, see?"

Mr. Cardini looked while Sidney pointed to the axe under the grave.

"Oh!" Mr. Cardini exclaimed. Then he turned to Miss Mackle who was trying not to laugh. "I think you have a great mural here. Put it up in the hallway. It will be a gift of peace and love to all!"

Harry flashed a big smile when the principal said *love*. Then he looked at Song Lee.

Song Lee went to her desk and took out a pencil and paper.

Then she folded it in half and gave it to Harry. Harry read it, and then he showed it to me:

Dear Harry
Remember your a, b, c, d Letter? My answer is c.

Song Lee

I remembered the *c* answer. That meant Song Lee liked Harry a lot! Harry was beaming. He took out his red foil present and walked over to the science table. Song Lee was alone. She was feeding Bong his daily liver.

I watched her open up the present. She unfolded the red foil paper carefully. She saved the bow. When she took the lid off the box, she smiled and said thank you. It was a necklace with a thin gold ribbon strung around five burnt-out Christmas tree lights.

Harry put it over her head. Then he came up to me. "What do you think of that gift I made?" he whispered.

"I think you're getting too mushy."

Horrible Harry didn't think so. He just flashed his pearly-whites at me.

Frogs, Liver, and Love?

Later that morning while our mural was drying, Miss Mackle said, "Now we are going to sketch each other. I hope you put in lots of detail."

"Can we pick who we draw?" Ida asked.

"No," Miss Mackle said. "Since the desks are close together I just want you to sketch whoever is next to you."

Harry beamed. His desk was pushed next to Song Lee's by the window.

Mine was near Ida's.

"I'm not near anyone!" Sidney complained. "I don't have a partner."

Miss Mackle quickly looked at the situation. "We'll have one group of three. Why don't you join Harry and Song Lee?"

"Yeah! I get to draw Harry!" Sidney cackled.

"That's fine," Miss Mackle agreed. "Harry is drawing Song Lee, and Song Lee will draw you, Sidney."

When the teacher placed a big sheet of white art paper on my desk, she said, "Doug, don't forget to draw Ida's beautiful black curls."

I frowned. Drawing curls was not my idea of a good time.

After she passed out paper, she said,

"Find out what the person that you are drawing likes and draw those things around the border."

Harry made a toothy smile as he started to sketch Song Lee. Sidney cackled as he looked at Harry and pulled out a pencil. Song Lee drew a big oval for Sidney's head.

"What do you like, Ida?" I asked.

"Ballet and music. What about you, Doug?"

"That's easy. I like Indians—Cochise, Sitting Bull, Geronimo "— I was running out of names so I threw one in from an old TV program, —"and Tonto."

"I can draw good Indian headbands with lots of feathers. I'll put them all around your portrait."

I didn't mind the assignment so much anymore. I just wondered what ballet shoes looked like. All I could remember was one pair in a shop window. They had long pink shoelaces.

"Can I borrow your pink?" I asked Song Lee. She had a box of 64 crayons.

When she handed me the pink, I looked at her drawing. She gave Sidney lots of hair and made it stick out. She put canary stickers and Tinkertoys in the border.

When I looked at Sidney's portrait of Harry I laughed! He put a moustache and beard on Harry's face. Now he was making horns.

Ol' Sidney was up to his tricks again.

At the moment, Harry was too busy to notice. He was drawing frogs, beetles, and liver on toothpicks around Song Lee's face.

It was a portrait of love all right.

"These are wonderful!" Miss Mackle exclaimed. When she got to Sidney's drawing, she frowned. "I didn't know Harry had hair on his face and was growing horns," she said.

The class laughed.

Harry held up his fist.

Sidney started erasing the moustache and beard. "I was just fooling around, Miss Mackle. I'll start over again."

"And why did you put canaries in the border? Harry likes dinosaurs and ants and . . ."

Harry looked at Song Lee.

Her face turned the same color as the crayon she was holding, carnation pink.

"And . . . ?" Sidney needed help.

"I like frogs, beetles, and liver," Harry replied.

Sidney got busy coloring.

"And my teeth!" Harry added.

Sidney looked up. "Your teeth?"

Harry flashed a big smile. "Two perfect rows of pearly-whites!"

Everyone laughed again. The teacher moved on while Sidney drew lots of teeth in the border. They reminded me of that cat's smile in *Alice in Wonderland*.

Harry went back to his drawing.

Song Lee made a little red heart on a piece of paper and gave it to Harry. I think she was glad Harry didn't punch Sidney's schnozzola.

I had to get back to more serious business. Drawing black curls and pink shoelaces.

Harry the Thief?

Something must have happened to Harry over the weekend. I didn't know what it was, but it sure made Harry act different.

Monday morning, Harry didn't flash his pearly-whites once!

Not even at Song Lee.

"Are you okay?" I asked in class.

Harry looked at me but he didn't say anything.

"So, you're giving me the silent treatment, huh?"

Harry didn't say a word.

He *was* giving me the silent treatment.

"Fine!" I said. "I'll just read about Indian shelters." Then I looked at some pictures of teepees, hogans, longhouses, and pueblos.

Song Lee stopped by Harry's desk with a piece of paper. "It is a picture of Bong," she said.

Harry just pushed the drawing away and put his head down.

Maybe Harry wasn't in love anymore?

I really didn't care if he was or wasn't. I just wanted him to be his old horrible self again.

Even Sidney noticed the way Harry was acting. He tried to tease him. "Hi, Harry the canary. What's the matter, El Tweeto?"

Harry didn't even hold up his fist. He took out a book about Tyrannosaurus Rex and started reading.

"Harry's no fun anymore," Sidney said, during library time. "He doesn't get bugged when I tease him and he doesn't chase me anymore."

42

Song Lee looked sad. "I think Harry is hurting inside."

"Maybe he should see the nurse with the alligator purse," Sidney cackled.

"He doesn't feel good in his heart," Song Lee said.

"Yeah," I agreed. "Something is bothering him. Maybe something happened at home."

Suddenly Sidney stopped cackling. "Maybe his parents are getting a divorce. Mine did last year. I felt sad for a long time."

I looked at Sidney. He never told us that before. "Who do you live with?" I asked.

"My dad. My mom just left us."

"I'm sorry about that, Sidney," I said.

"Me, too," Song Lee said.

"Well," Sidney replied. "If Harry's

mom left, we could tell by looking at his lunch."

"That's right!" I said. "Harry's mom always packs something homemade in his lunchbox. If there's nothing homemade in there, she's probably gone."

At noontime, we all sat next to Harry.

We watched him take out a peanut butter sandwich, a banana, and . . .

Three pieces of homemade fudge!

"She's still here!" I called out.

Harry looked at me funny as he gave me a piece of fudge, Song Lee a piece, and Sidney a piece.

Now I *really* knew something was wrong. Harry didn't leave a piece for himself.

What was making Harry feel so horrible?

We got our first clue during math.

Just when Harry was getting his workbook, two dollars fell out of his desk.

Two dollars!

It was not a day to bring in lunch money. It was not a bake-sale day.

Where did Harry get that money?

Did he steal it? I pictured Harry on a WANTED poster down at the post office. It was horrible.

My best friend a robber? *A thief!*

I *had* to find out what was the matter with Harry during two-o'clock recess. As soon as I spotted him, I jumped on his back and knocked him over in the snow. After I pinned him down, I shouted, "TELL ME WHAT IS GOING ON OR I'LL . . ."

Sidney joined in, "OR YOU'LL SMASH HIS SCHNOZZ."

I held up my fist and acted like I was going to do it. Song Lee came running over. "NO FIGHTING!" she shouted. When she kneeled next to Harry, she said, "We will just talk like friends."

"He won't talk," Sidney grumbled.

"He won't talk," I said.

"He *will* talk," Song Lee said. "Give him a chance."

I stopped pinning Harry down, and got off him.

Harry sat up and looked at all of us. He looked like he was going to cry.

"You want the horrible truth?" he said.

We all nodded.

"It happened Saturday night. I knocked them both out when I ran into a wall. See?"

Harry opened his mouth wide.

We all looked inside.

Harry's two front teeth were missing.

I felt bad.

Song Lee handed Harry her handkerchief with the pink cherry blossoms on it. Harry blew his nose and gave it back to her.

Sidney patted Harry's back. "It happens to every second grader. My front teeth are *both* wiggly."

"You'll get new permanent ones," I said. I didn't know how important

Harry's teeth were to him.

Harry rubbed his finger along his gum where the empty spaces were.

"Grandfather Bong lost his permanent teeth," Song Lee said. "That is *really* sad."

Harry stood up. "Hey! I feel something rough in my gum!"

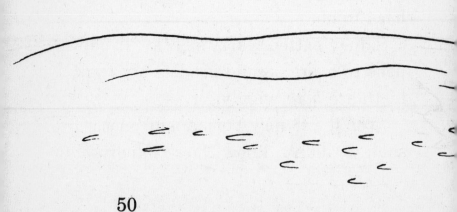

We all looked into his mouth again. "You're getting new teeth!" I said.

"NEW TEETH!" Harry shouted. He jumped up and down so many times he made a deep hole in the snowbank.

The three of us had to pull him out!

"Want to get some doughnuts after school at the corner bakery?" Harry

said, holding up two dollars. "I have my tooth-fairy money."

Boy, was I relieved! My best friend wasn't a robber after all.

"SURE!" we shouted.

Sometimes when we share the horrible truth, we become closer friends.

ABOUT THE AUTHOR

Suzy Kline graduated from the University of California at Berkeley and received her elementary school teacher's credential from California State University at Hayward. She has been teaching for sixteen years and is the author of the popular Herbie Jones series (available in Puffin). Kline was selected Teacher of the Year in 1986 by the Torrington School District in Connecticut and in 1988 by the Probus Club of Torrington. Kline is married and has two daughters.